School of Rock

COME TOGETHER

School of Rock

COME TOGETHER

adapted by Mary Tillworth
based on the teleplay by Jim Armogida,
Steve Armogida, and Mike White

SCHOLASTIC INC.

CHAPTER 1

IT WAS MOMENTS BEFORE THE FIRST bell at William Travis Preparatory School, and Freddy was on an important mission. "From the front of the school to the classroom in thirty seconds!" he announced into his GoPro camera. He tightened the camera around his skateboarding helmet, being careful not to rub the straps against the grinning skull decal.

Jamming his helmet over his thick brown hair, Freddy dropped his skateboard onto the pavement and checked his chunky red wristwatch. He clicked on the stopwatch, stepped

onto the skateboard's scratchy black grip tape, and pushed off.

The plastic green wheels rumbled through the parking lot, jerking to a halt in front of a concrete staircase. Freddy flipped the skateboard under his arm and climbed the steps up to the school entrance. He pushed the doors open. They barely had a chance to swing shut before he was back on his skateboard and coasting down the hallway.

When he came to an intersection, he made a sharp right turn, skating over the school's emblem—a shield bearing a scroll and quill feather, an open book, a compass, and the state of Texas with a star planted over the city of Austin. The school's name and the year it was established—1949—was written in formal block letters around the shield.

Freddy ollied down a small flight of stairs and sped through the hallway, dodging students

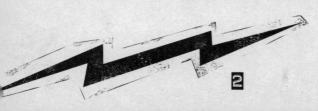

left and right. As he passed his classmates Summer and Tomika, he gave Summer a wink.

Summer tossed her blonde hair back and clutched her notebooks to her chest. "I am *not* impressed," she called as Freddy rolled past.

After Freddy rounded the corner, Summer turned to Tomika. "I am *so* impressed!" she squealed. Her blue eyes shined with excitement. She had been crushing on Freddy ever since the beginning of the school year.

Tomika looked up from stuffing her backpack with textbooks. She hadn't even seen Freddy go by.

"What do you think of Freddy?" Summer asked excitedly.

Tomika shrugged. She was a skateboarder, too. "Eh. Decent kick flip. Wicked railslide." She slammed her locker shut and hefted her binders under her arm. "But I'd have to see him on the half pipe before judging him."

"Can't you just say he's cute, like a normal person?" Summer grasped the side of her locker door, which was covered in magazine clippings and pink decorations. Positive sayings like SOAR and ON TOP OF THE WORLD were strewn everywhere.

"He's cute. Are you happy?" grumbled Tomika. But she wasn't really grumpy. She and Summer had been BFFs since second grade, and Tomika was used to her friend going gaga over boys.

Summer beamed. She closed her locker and the two girls headed to class.

Meanwhile, Freddy was gaining speed as he approached the classroom. Girls screamed as they fled out of the path of his skateboard. "Watch out, Zack!" he warned as he zoomed by a well-dressed Asian kid wearing a gray prep suit and a dark blue tie.

"Whoa, Freddy!" Zack pulled his tie out of the way just in time.

With one final push, Freddy burst into the classroom and checked his stopwatch. "Twenty-eight seconds. New record!" he crowed.

"I built this rocket in record time, too," bragged the sandy-haired kid, Lawrence. He was dressed in a red blazer and wore thick black glasses. He held up a simple model rocket that resembled an oversized crayon with wings. "Eight months!"

Freddy raised his eyebrows. Eight months didn't seem like a record to him.

The kid looked down at his rocket. "It's not a fast sport," he mumbled.

Just then, Zack came through the classroom door. He immediately spotted the model rocket and shook his head. "Lawrence, you'd better hide that. You know rockets are against the rules."

"Freddy should get in more trouble than me," Lawrence protested. "He just skated down the hallway like he was in a body spray commercial." He heard the sound of authoritative footsteps approaching the door and quickly hid the rocket under the desk.

An older woman wearing a striped pink button-up dress shirt and a gray tweed skirt entered the room—their teacher, Mrs. Calpakis. Summer and Tomika scrambled in behind her, hastily taking their seats.

Freddy looked around for a place to stash his skateboard, but it was too late.

"Freddy!" the woman said. "Skateboarding is against school rules."

"Hello, Mrs. Calpakis. You look lovely today!" said Freddy.

"Why, thank you!" Mrs. Calpakis preened. "It's just a little something I put togeth—" She frowned and folded her arms. "Nice try sweet

talking me." She reached out and took the skateboard. "This is going in the Confiscation Closet. Someone could get hurt!"

Freddy groaned. The Confiscation Closet was the worst. Any item Mrs. Calpakis found that she thought to be dangerous or a nuisance or even slightly against school rules went directly into it. Students considered themselves lucky if their confiscated possessions were given back to them at the end of the year.

"Can't you just be chill about this?" pleaded Freddy.

"Oh, I'm more chill than you think. In fact, I used to roller boogie!" Mrs. Calpakis set the skateboard on the floor. She hopped aboard and shoved off—a little too hard.

The students watched in horror as their teacher careened across the classroom. Waving her arms wildly, she lost her balance and crashed hard into her own desk. She flipped into the air and landed with a thump onto the floor.

"Ow," a voice whispered from below the chalkboard.

"She is *not* good at roller boogie," said Lawrence.

CHAPTER 2

"I APPRECIATE YOU BEING ABLE TO STEP

in on such late notice." Principal Mullins's high heels clicked briskly as she led the students' new substitute teacher down the hall. The principal was a tall, thin, prim woman with stylish ebony glasses and straight red hair pulled neatly back from her face.

"I do it all for the kids," said the substitute teacher, almost dropping his bag as he struggled to keep up. He laughed nervously and ran a hand through his long, scraggly blonde hair. "Um, will I be paid in advance?"

Principal Mullins raised her eyebrows. "You will get a check at the end of the week." She opened the door to the classroom and marched inside. "Hello, children," she said sternly.

The students scrambled to their seats. They clasped their hands and sat as properly as they could. "Helloooo, Principal Mullins," they droned. They knew from experience that any hint of unruliness would be punished by immediate detention.

"Mrs. Calpakis broke her hip and will be out indefinitely." Principal Mullins gestured toward the unkempt man who had stumbled in after her. "This is your new substitute, Mr. Finn."

The students looked at Mr. Finn curiously. He didn't seem like the usual William Travis Prep substitute teacher. His hair was too messy. The back of his tie was showing. Underneath his schoolteacher's blazer, he was wearing an

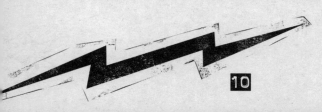

unzipped hoodie. The hoodie strings were sticking out.

Mr. Finn gave the class a thumbs-up sign. Only Summer gave him a small thumbs-up back.

Principal Mullins picked up a piece of chalk and wrote Mr. Finn's name in large neat letters on the board. "Please be courteous and respectful."

Mr. Finn nodded vigorously. "I will try."

Principal Mullins looked confused. "I was speaking to the children."

Mr. Finn giggled nervously and bared his teeth in an awkward smile.

Principal Mullins shook her head and strode toward the door. Before she pushed it open, she leaned over and spoke in a confidential tone to Mr. Finn. "FYI, the students in your class are . . . gifted."

"We'll see about that," scoffed Mr. Finn. "What's three times four?" he yelled suddenly.

"Twelve," the entire class replied.

Mr. Finn was amazed. "I guess you're right!"

Principal Mullins rolled her eyes and left, not noticing the peace sign that Mr. Finn gave to her as she click-clacked away.

Mr. Finn threw his bag onto the teacher's desk and faced the room. He saw well-disciplined students in uniforms sitting in straight rows. Every single desk was impeccably tidy—there was no hint of creative mess anywhere. Classroom posters hung at perfect angles from the walls. Even the books on the bookcases had been carefully arranged so that nothing stuck out or was even remotely out of place.

"Let's rock and roll, young learners!" Mr. Finn picked up the attendance list that was attached to a clipboard. "Okay, roll call. Dig it!" He decided that he was going to begin the class by making things a little fun. He dropped the list. "I'm gonna give you all awesome nicknames." He clapped his hands together and started pointing. "Hot Rod! Clapton! Gooch! Axl Rose . . . if he was a girl!" He aimed a finger at Summer. "Headband!"

Summer touched her headband self-consciously. No one had ever given her a nickname before. She raised her hand. "But . . . my name is Summer."

"Dude, you can't give yourself a nickname." Mr. Finn pointed to Tomika. "You'll be Summer."

Tomika's eyes widened. She wasn't so sure of the new substitute teacher. He wasn't making a lot of sense. "This is gonna be really confusing," she groaned.

"Dr. Roboto!" Mr. Finn shouted to Lawrence.

Lawrence grinned uneasily.

"Zack!" yelled Mr. Finn, pointing to the next kid.

"But that's my actual name," said Zack.

"Your parents nailed it!" Mr. Finn said. He finished shouting nicknames to the rest of the class and went to his desk to find the lesson plan for the day.

While Mr. Finn rummaged inside his bag, Lawrence took the opportunity to fiddle with the controls of his rocket. He had finished assembling it only last night, and still wasn't exactly sure if it worked. He was pressing buttons randomly, trying to figure out what buttons did what, when the rocket abruptly launched off his desk. Lawrence tried to grab it, but it was too late. The rocket shot toward the front of the classroom, heading straight for Mr. Finn.

Mr. Finn whirled around. The rocket zoomed by in a cloud of bright blue smoke, narrowly missing his face before crashing into

the Good Behavior Pledge poster next to the chalkboard.

Lawrence sank into his seat, the controller frozen in his hands. He was sure that his rocket was doomed for the Confiscation Closet.

CHAPTER 3

"WHO DID THAT?" DEMANDED MR. FINN.

The class stayed quiet. Lawrence sank even lower in his chair.

Mr. Finn bent down and gingerly picked up the rocket. Once he was certain that it wasn't going to explode on him, he grinned and held it high. "Because. That. Was. Awesome!"

Lawrence breathed a sigh of relief. He could barely believe his luck. "So you're not going to put it in the Confiscation Closet?"

"New teacher, new rules." Mr. Finn set down the rocket. "I say let's make this whole learning

thing fun!" He leaned against a binder on the teacher's desk. "I don't just want to teach you guys, I wanna inspi—aaaahhh!" The binder slid to the floor, with Mr. Finn close behind.

"All I'm saying," continued Mr. Finn as he stood up and brushed himself off, "is that we can do this the boring way, or the Mr. Finn way."

Zack's eyes lit up. He looked around at the other students. Everyone else looked excited. The new teacher was definitely more fun than Mrs. Calpakis!

Mr. Finn spotted a plastic skull perched at the edge of the teacher's desk. He picked it up and moved the jaw up and down to make it speak. "I say we do it the Mr. Finn way!" he said in a high-pitched squeak.

Zack raised his hand. "I'm in!" he shouted.

Summer's hand shot up faster than lightning. "Me, too!" She smiled happily. "Freddy

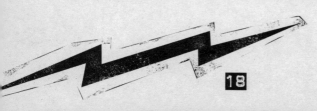

and I are in." Already she was dreaming about all the other things that she and Freddy would agree on.

Tomika grabbed the sides of her desk and grinned. "If Headband's in, I'm in!"

All the other students nodded their heads.

"Great!" Mr. Finn put the skull down and plunged his hands into his teacher's bag. "Because I snuck a box of doughnuts . . . from the teachers' lounge!" His hands emerged holding a large pink bakery box. He opened the box and showed the students what was inside. The box was stuffed with every kind of doughnut that they could imagine.

"Guys, we just won the substitute teacher lottery!" Zack made a beeline for the dough-nuts, with the other students crowding behind him. They grabbed frosted sprinkled dough-nuts, Bavarian cream doughnuts, powdered doughnuts, glazed doughnuts, and chocolate covered doughnuts. Lawrence tilted his head back and guzzled as he squeezed out the contents of a strawberry jelly doughnut.

In a few seconds flat, the classroom had turned into a raucous, sugar-fueled dance party. Students got up on their chairs and whirled and spun and gobbled doughnuts. Summer and Tomika took turns feeding each other frosted sprinkle doughnuts.

Zack threw handfuls of doughnut holes in the air. One of them bounced off of Summer's teeth. Another hit Tomika's chin. Lawrence got whacked in the nose. But Zack and Mr. Finn managed to nab a doughnut hole. With their mouths full, they raised their hands and high fived each other.

By the end of the doughnut party, the students were back at their seats, their faces covered in chocolate and jelly and frosting. They were so happy.

"That was the best two minutes of my entire life!" Lawrence sighed, his mouth smeared with powder and jam.

The other students nodded dazedly in agreement.

Lawrence held up a finger. "I'm crashing." His head thumped down onto his desk.

"Best sub ever," Tomika whispered to Summer. But she still had her reservations. Even though the first couple minutes with Mr. Finn had been incredible, she couldn't believe that they had gotten so lucky. "There's gotta be a catch."

CHAPTER 4

"ALL RIGHT. IT SAYS HERE Y'ALL ARE discussing sonnets by William Shakespeare." Mr. Finn thumbed through the lesson plan that Mrs. Calpakis had left. The lessons were far more complicated than he remembered from when he was in the seventh grade.

Summer nodded. She thought back to English class from the other day, when Mrs. Calpakis had tried to explain Shakespeare to the students. Half of them had fallen asleep. The ones who had managed to stay awake still weren't sure that the words coming out of

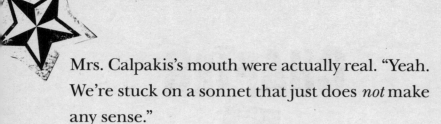

Mrs. Calpakis's mouth were actually real. "Yeah. We're stuck on a sonnet that just does *not* make any sense."

Mr. Finn put down the lesson plan and picked up the book of Shakespeare's sonnets. "Well, you can always tell everything you need to know about a poem from its title." He paged through the book until he found the right sonnet. "This is called . . . Sonnet 137." He looked up at the class, a little uncomfortably. Apparently Shakespeare didn't think that poem titles were that important. "That's—deep," he said, trying to save himself.

Summer furrowed her eyebrows. She didn't understand why the title was deep, and she had a feeling that the new substitute didn't, either. But she was willing to give him a shot. He had, after all, brought the entire class doughnuts.

Mr. Finn cleared his throat and began to read. "Thy blind fool, Love, what dost thou

to mine eyes." He shook his head, as if clearing cobwebs from his eyes. "Maybe it'll make more sense in a British accent." He tried again. "Thy blind fool, Love, what dost thou to mine eyes?"

The class stared at him blankly.

"Nope." Mr. Finn gulped.

"I knew there was a catch." Tomika leaned over to Summer. Her suspicions were right. "This teacher can't teach," she whispered.

Just then, the second period bell rang.

Mr. Finn's shoulders sagged with relief. "Wow, that was fast!" He shut the book and grabbed his bag. "Great day, guys! We'll get to the bottom of this sonnet tomorrow."

Summer got out of her seat. "Um, it's only ten. We're just going to music class."

Mr. Finn smiled weakly. He set his bag back down as the students filed out. "Riiiiight." As the last kid shuffled through the class-room door, he let out a gigantic sigh. He had

survived his first class, and the students hadn't caught on yet that he wasn't a real teacher. He just hoped that he would make it to the end of the day.

Mr. Finn didn't have class for the next forty-five minutes, so he figured it was a good time to explore. He left the classroom and started to roam around the school. As he wandered down a hallway, he heard classical music. The piece was being played extremely well, with each note ringing true.

Mr. Finn loved music. He preferred rock and roll, but he loved listening to talented musicians play—even classical. He followed the sound to the music room and peeked inside.

Lawrence was on the piano, playing each chord with beautiful precision. Tomika slid a bow across a cello, the deep notes echoing across the room. The melodic sweet tones of the clarinet came from Summer, while Freddy waited patiently until it was his turn to gently clang the cymbals. Zack plucked at a guitar, creating a perfect medley of sound.

As he watched the students, Mr. Finn smiled. "I think I just found a way to teach these guys." He dashed outside the school and threw open the doors to his van. Scattered inside were all the instruments for a rock band—an electric keyboard, tons of guitars, a full drum set, a tambourine, and maracas. There were half a dozen amps and plenty of cables to hook them to the electric instruments. Yellow and red twinkle lights lined the edges of the van.

Mr. Finn grabbed his keyboard, two guitars, the tambourine, and an armful of cables. He rushed back to his classroom, slowing down only in front of other classrooms so he didn't raise suspicion. He only had a few minutes left, and he wanted his plan to be in place for when the students returned.

CHAPTER 5

WHEN THE STUDENTS WALKED BACK

into Mr. Finn's classroom, they stopped short. Everything had been transformed!

The desks, which were usually lined in neat straight rows, had been shoved aside. A drum set stood in the back corner with a microphone rigged above it. A long cable ran from an amp to an electric keyboard. Mr. Finn was fiddling with an electric guitar, which was hooked up to another amp. A Nirvana poster hung from the chalkboard in the back. The room looked like it could be the stage for a rock concert!

"Wait. What did you do to our classroom?" gasped Summer.

"He made it awesome!" cried Freddy. He was digging Mr. Finn more and more!

"I heard you all in music class. You guys are good!" Mr. Finn grabbed a pick. "And I realized there's a better way to learn Shakespeare—by adding a little rock and roll!" He brought his pick to the guitar strings and strummed.

A wild chord echoed across the room. It didn't sound like anything they had ever played in music class!

Mr. Finn strode over to Zack. "Ever play electric guitar?" he asked.

"No. My father makes me play classical." Zack held up a finger. "He says that music should be boring."

"Mmm. Wroooong." Mr. Finn handed the electric guitar to Zack. It had blue lightning zigzagged across the strap. "Hit me with some Beethoven."

Zack put on the guitar. It was the coolest instrument that he had ever touched! Fingers trembling, he timidly started to play "Für Elise." When he got to the last note of the first phrase, Mr. Finn slammed a foot down on a distortion pedal. Beethoven unleashed through the classroom like a screaming eagle.

"That was awesome!" yelled Zack.

Mr. Finn picked up a sleek white electric bass guitar. "Tomika. That cello you're playing has four strings, right?"

Tomika nodded. "Uh-huh."

"So does this bass." Mr. Finn slung the guitar over Tomika's head.

Tomika took a deep breath and started to pick a sweet riff on the bass. Her hand glided over the strings as if she was born to jam. *If only playing the cello was this much fun!* she thought.

"Welcome to Funkytown—population you, lady!" laughed Mr. Finn.

Tomika grinned. "Oh, yeah. I'm bringing on the funk!"

Mr. Finn pointed. "Lawrence. How long have you been playing the piano?"

Lawrence darted to the keyboard. He couldn't wait to prove his skills to Mr. Finn. "Since I was eleven months old!"

"Okay, your parents are pushing you a little too hard, but that's a problem for another day." Mr. Finn cued Lawrence. "Right now, you're on keys."

Lawrence raised his hand to rock and roll. But just as he was about to play, Mr. Finn called out: "But first, mess up your hair. You look like a LEGO guy."

Lawrence shoved his hands in his hair and rubbed frantically. When he was done, his hair

stuck out crazily, as though he had just been electrocuted.

Mr. Finn nodded approvingly. "Now you look like a rock star."

Lawrence ran his hand over the keys, ending with a ferocious chord.

"All right. We need a drummer." Mr. Finn surveyed the remaining students. "Freddy. Think you can handle it?"

Freddy ran to the drum set and picked up the drumsticks. "I don't know, Mr. Finn," he said. He sat down and looked down at the drums uncertainly.

Mr. Finn gave Freddy an encouraging smile. He had only seen Freddy on the cymbals, but he had a feeling he would be a natural on the drums.

Freddy took a deep breath. He lifted the sticks—and played a killer rhythm in perfect

time. What Mr. Finn didn't know was that Freddy had been taking drum lessons for years.

Summer gazed at Freddy with absolute adoration. Not only was he cute, he was a cute drummer!

"Yeah. I got this," Freddy said with a grin.

"Summer." Mr. Finn held up the book of sonnets. "Can you read the poem?"

"You *know*-em," said Summer, trying—and failing—to sound cool.

Mr. Finn raised his eyebrows.

"Just give me the book," Summer muttered. She grabbed it from Mr. Finn and took her place in front of the microphone. She was sure that as soon as she read the poem, Freddy would fall in love with her.

"I reread that sonnet and realized what it really is," said Mr. Finn. He looked around the class. "It's an angry break-up song!"

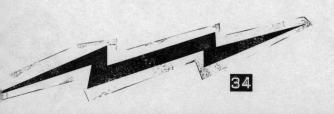

"Oh! So, like a Taylor Swift song," said Summer. She knew exactly what Mr. Finn was talking about. She opened the book of poetry and found Sonnet 137.

"Okay. Um, sure!" agreed Mr. Finn. He draped an electric guitar around his neck. "Sonnets have a rhyme scheme, so let's put it to music. Follow my lead."

CHAPTER 6

MR. FINN PLAYED A CHORD ON THE
guitar. It was low and angry and tense. He kept
the chord going, strumming it over and over as
Freddy kept the beat on the drums.

Summer read the first line of the sonnet. "Thy blind fool, Love, what dost thou to
mine eyes."

"In rock, that means . . ." Mr. Finn turned
up the volume and the group rocked.

> *"Love isn't kind*
> *It makes you blind!"*

Tomika leaned back as she thrummed on the bass.

"That they behold, and see not what they see?" continued Summer.

*"I thought you were hot
And now I know you're not!"*

"Smoke machine!" Mr. Finn yelled.

One of the students scampered to the middle of the classroom with Mr. Finn's smoke machine. In a few seconds, smoke was pouring over the floor and onto the musicians.

"Lights!" commanded Mr. Finn.

Another student switched on the strobe lights. The classroom was covered in swirling pulses of yellow, red, and blue.

"Tasty lead!" shouted Mr. Finn. His fingers danced over the guitar, and a red-hot rock solo burst forth. "Skip down to the last bit!" he yelled.

Summer's eyes darted to the bottom of the page. "In things right true my heart and eyes have erred, And to this false plague are they now transferred."

"I got this," shouted Freddy. He was actually getting Shakespeare—in a language he could understand!

"I'm crushing on a girl and it's a major bummer!"

"Yeah, that's it," said Mr. Finn. He paused for a second. "But my lyrics rhymed." He built the music up to the finale. "Keys!"

Lawrence wailed on the keyboard.

"Drum fill!" shouted Mr. Finn.

Freddy put his head down and banged away with all his might.

"Bring us home, Tomika!" yelled Mr. Finn.

Tomika reared back as she finished the song with one final sweet riff.

"Yeah!" Mr. Finn high fived the class. "All right!"

"Wow. Shakespeare rocked the funk!" cried Tomika.

"Where did you learn to teach like that?" Zack asked Mr. Finn. He had no idea that English class could be so much fun, or have so much music in it!

"Uhhh, I'm in a special program," stuttered Mr. Finn. "I'm, uh, getting my master's in, uh, Teachology at the . . . Van Halen Institute. I go every day after school."

This was it. Mr. Finn was sure the students would know that he wasn't a real teacher. But just then, the school bell rang.

Mr. Finn sighed happily and took off his

guitar. He laid it across the teacher's desk and picked up his bag to go. "Great day, guys!"

Summer shook her head. "It's just lunchtime."

"Seriously?" moaned Mr. Finn. He set down his bag for the second time. "Man, I really need to get a watch."

CHAPTER 7

AFTER CLASS, THE STUDENTS ALL MET

on the school steps to discuss their first day with their new substitute teacher.

"Mr. Finn is fun," said Tomika, "but there's no way he's a real teacher." She shook her head. "He asked to borrow lunch money."

"Okay, maybe he doesn't follow rules, steals doughnuts, and calls us dudes, but that doesn't mean . . ." Zack sighed, accepting Tomika's logic. "Yeah, he's not a real teacher," he said sadly.

"If he's not for real, we might not graduate,"

Summer groaned. Middle school was hard, but she *had* to make it through. She looked down at herself. "I don't think I could survive on the streets!"

"Guys. He's the best teacher we've ever had." Freddy slung his backpack over a shoulder. "Just because he's fun doesn't mean he's not legit." He took off down the school steps. "I'll prove it."

The gang watched as Freddy started running down the street. They knew if their friend was determined to prove something, he would. They folded their arms and waited for him to return with evidence that Mr. Finn was a real teacher.

A few seconds later, Freddy was back. "You guys were supposed to come with me."

"Ohhhhh," everyone said. They followed Freddy off the school grounds and into the city.

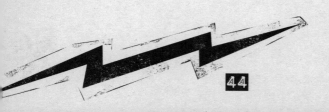

That evening, a crowd gathered at the dingy entrance of a large brick building. It was a music club, where local Austin bands came to play gigs. Next to the open door, a neon red guitar sign hung above a spray painted metal trashcan. ROCK & ROLL was written in more neon, splashed across the middle of the guitar. Next to the sign, LIVE MUSIC flashed on and off in electric blue.

Five students from William Travis Prep dodged through the crowd and scooted inside the club. They looked around, taking in the foggy room, the grungy kids in punk clothes, the flashing purple lights that pulsed to the music being played on the stage.

"So far we've followed Mr. Finn to a taco

truck and laser tag." Summer had to shout above the deafening music in order to be heard. "And now here...?" Her voice trailed off as she saw a familiar face on the stage. It was Mr. Finn. He was wearing an unzipped black sweatshirt and a brown T-shirt, banging his head back and forth, an electric guitar strapped to his side. He was rocking out!

"That's our teacher?" shouted Freddy in disbelief.

"Dewey Finn? Teacher?" A guy in a red and gray plaid shirt turned to Freddy and laughed hysterically. "He's not qualified to teach a dog to bark!" He lifted his hands in rocker mode. "But he is a Rock. God. Whoo!" The guy turned back to the stage with crazed eyes.

Mr. Finn flung his guitar to his bandmate. "Rock and roll!" he yelled as he leapt off the stage. But instead of bodysurfing, he landed with a gigantic thud on the sticky club floor.

When he looked up, Freddy, Summer, Tomika, Zack, and Lawrence were staring at him. "Oh. Hey guys," he said, giving them a pained little wave.

"Definitely not a teacher," said Freddy, shaking his head. He had finally been convinced.

CHAPTER 8

THE NEXT MORNING, THE STUDENTS bunched together in small groups, talking about whether or not they should turn Mr. Finn in to Principal Mullins. Even though the previous day had been awesome, they knew for certain now that he was a fraud. No teacher at William Travis Preparatory School would be caught dead inside a rock club, let alone be the main act.

"Morning, class!" Mr. Finn greeted his students as he walked into the room.

Everyone stopped talking and quietly

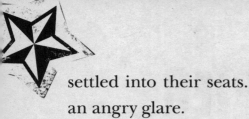

settled into their seats. Tomika shot Mr. Finn
an angry glare.

"Oh I get it." Mr. Finn took off his bag and
leaned against the side of the teacher's desk.
He folded his arms. "The silent treatment."

"We're mad at you!" shouted Lawrence.

Zack turned to Lawrence and put a finger
to his lips. "Shhh!"

"What?" Lawrence held his hands up help-
lessly. "I'm not good at the silent treatment."

Zack turned back to the front of the room
with an exasperated sigh.

"And Zack, I'm still mad at you for drinking
my smoothie in the third grade," continued
Lawrence.

Zack turned around again.

Lawrence raised his arms. "I'm getting it all
out, people!"

Summer raised her eyebrows, but didn't
say anything. She was less concerned with

Lawrence's feelings and more concerned that the person standing in front of them could be a serious threat to her ability to graduate.

"I'm sorry I lied to you," said Mr. Finn.

"You're not even a real teacher." Summer couldn't keep the disappointment out of her voice.

Mr. Finn dropped his head. "You're right. Until two days ago, I worked at my uncle's yogurt stand on Sixth Street during the day, and tried to be a rock star at night." He looked out the window, reminiscing about all the great times he'd had. "Playing gigs. Staying out late. Thousands of people screaming my name." He hesitated. "Well, more like thirty. But still."

"That sounds awesome!" said Zack.

Mr. Finn nodded. "Yeah. My whole world was trying to win Battle of the Bands."

Tomika folded her arms across her desk. Even though she wasn't sure about having Mr.

Finn as a teacher, she did like the fact that he had let them play some incredible music. And she was curious. "What's Battle of the Bands?"

Mr. Finn crouched in front of Tomika. His eyes glittered with excitement. "It's this epic contest with all the best bands in Austin," he explained. "If your band wins, you become legendary!"

Despite herself, Tomika's face broke into a huge smile. That sounded so rad!

"But I gave all that up," said Mr. Finn. He straightened up and faced the class. "Last night was my last gig."

"Why?" asked Freddy.

Mr. Finn thought for a moment. "Because I'm at that stage of my life where I want something real."

"Something real . . ." Tomika wrinkled her eyebrows. She wasn't quite following Mr. Finn. "Like . . . fake teaching?"

Mr. Finn shook his head. "Look. My mom's a substitute teacher, and she loves it. So I fibbed about my qualifications to get this job. And you know what?" He smiled. "I love it, too! Being your teacher is way cooler than playing at any club. And that's the truth."

There was a long silence as the students looked at one another. They knew that in the next few moments, they would have to decide how the rest of the year was going to go—the normal, boring, William Travis Prep way, or the Mr. Finn way.

Mr. Finn picked up the plastic skull and clacked its jaw up and down. "I say we forgive him." He looked at the students hopefully.

Summer stared down at her hands. As much as she liked Mr. Finn, she was worried that she wouldn't be able to graduate if she agreed to let him teach her. "We like you too, but we have to learn stuff."

"I'm sorry Mr. Finn, but we need a real teacher," agreed Tomika.

"I don't know, guys," Lawrence piped up. "The skull makes a strong argument."

Zack shot Lawrence a withering glare. "The skull's an idiot." He turned back to Mr. Finn. "My dad wants me to get into Yale."

"Are you going to turn me in?" Mr. Finn's shoulders hunched up, expecting the worst.

Freddy stood up. He had loved playing the drums in class, but he was also really angry that Mr. Finn had misled them. He had defended Mr. Finn, called him a real teacher, only to find that he and the rest of class had been lied to. Freddy could feel disappointment swelling up in his throat. "We don't know. But right now we have to go. Principal Mullins makes us play a recital in the quad once a month." He stormed past Mr. Finn and pulled opened the classroom door. "You know, what you did was not cool," he said.

The other students followed Freddy out into the hallway. As they passed Mr. Finn, none of them looked him in the eye.

Mr. Finn held the plastic skull up. It gazed at him reproachfully. "Don't look at me like that," he said.

CHAPTER 9

A SHORT WHILE LATER, CALM, SWEET,
and utterly uninspiring music filtered through
the quad. Students sat at red painted metal
tables, their chins propped up on their hands
in a desperate effort to stay awake. A few kids
were leaning against the exterior brick wall,
covering their mouths as their eyes drooped
lower and lower. As one long boring note came
after another, it seemed as though the recital
would never end.

The musicians weren't having much fun,
either. Zack slumped in a chair, picking tiredly

at his guitar. Freddy stood in front of the drums, his padded sticks tapping out a listless beat. Summer blew on the clarinet with no enthusiasm, while Tomika hunched forward as she played the cello. Lawrence wasn't even trying to sound good on the piano.

Principal Mullins stood in front of the group, her fingers waving in pleased little strokes to the time. Behind her, all the students were yawning and rolling their eyes at one another.

"I wish we could rock out like we did with Mr. Finn," Freddy whispered to Summer. Even though he was mad at their teacher, playing this dull music was seriously bumming him out.

"Principal Mullins would kill us!" Zack raised his head. "And my dad would kill me." His eyes widened. "I'd be dead—twice!"

Just then, Clark, the hall monitor, burst into the quad. His chest heaved frantically as he

gasped for air. He was a tiny kid with beady brown eyes, slicked back blond hair, and a goody-two-shoes attitude. His yellow safety vest was so bright, it blinded some of the students into waking up. "Principal Mullins, we have a situation," he announced in a breathless, high-pitched voice. "There's a 483 in progress."

Principal Mullins stiffened. "An atomic wedgie?" She snapped her head at Clark. "Let's roll." She strode back into the school, with Clark hot on her heels.

Summer stopped playing. "Principal Mullins is gone!" She had an idea. She was ready to make things a little more interesting. "We can do this the boring way . . . or the Mr. Finn way."

"Summer, do you know what I like about you?" asked Freddy.

Summer's heart jumped. This was it! Freddy was finally taking notice of her! "Is it my smile?

My eyes? The way I make you feel?" she asked, her voice squeaky with anticipation.

Freddy shook his head, confused. "I meant the song, 'What I Like About You.'"

"Oh! Yeah, me too," Summer babbled, trying her best to recover. "I mean, are those not the lyrics?"

Freddy gave her a strange look.

Summer winced.

Tomika spoke up quickly, trying to save her best friend from utter humiliation. "Let's do this!" she shouted. She frantically motioned for Freddy to start the song.

Freddy smiled and hit his sticks together. "One, two, three, four!"

Like magic, the band shook off their musty old recital music and started jamming. Tomika threw away her bow and began plucking at the strings of her cello. Lawrence played the

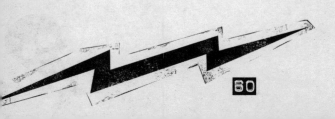

opening chords to the song as everyone started to sing.

It was as if a light had been switched on in the quad. The students shook themselves awake. They stood up and started to move in time with the beat.

Freddy looked up from the drums. *This is how music is supposed to be!* he thought to himself.

In no time at all, the students were laughing and dancing and clapping to the music. Tomika spun her cello and threw it sideways, playing it like an electric bass. Zack wailed away on his own guitar, matching her note for note.

When the song was finished, the crowd cheered and whistled and clapped. It had been the best recital at William Travis Prep ever!

Zack unslung his guitar and held it high in the air. "Good night, Austin!" he yelled.

CHAPTER 10

AFTER THE RECITAL, THE STUDENTS gathered around to talk. They were amazed at how good they had sounded together, and how they had been able to electrify the crowd with their rock and roll.

"We should start a band!" said Tomika.

"That would be so cool!" Summer was already thinking ten steps ahead. "Maybe if we're good enough, we can enter the Battle of the Bands."

"If we enter, we'll win!" Freddy said confidently.

Zack wasn't so sure. "Does anyone here

know anything about being in a rock band?" He hated to be the practical one, but he was almost certain that none of them knew much about rocking out—other than what Mr. Finn had taught them.

Lawrence hitched up the edges of his suit. "Yes!" He paused. "Oh. Rock band?" He shook his head and rubbed his eyeglasses. "No."

Tomika snapped her fingers. "Mr. Finn can help us! He knows all about rock and roll."

Zack was still skeptical. "Yeah, but there's no way Principal Mullins will let us play rock music in class."

"Then we'll keep it a secret." Freddy nodded, appreciating the genius of the idea. "Mr. Finn can help with that, too!"

"I'm so excited, I could hug you!" squealed Summer.

Freddy gave her a quizzical look.

"Allll. I could hug you all." Summer tried to

change the pitch of her voice so it wasn't so high and nervous.

"Bring it in, sister!" Lawrence went in for the squeeze, and wrapped Summer in a giant bear hug.

"Oof," said Summer.

With their plan in place, Freddy, Summer, Tomika, Zack, and Lawrence couldn't wait to tell Mr. Finn. They raced back to their classroom and charged through the door.

"Mr. Finn! We changed our mind!" Freddy shouted. He stopped and looked around. There was no one in sight. "Mr. Finn?"

The students glanced at the teacher's desk. They saw a giant cardboard box on it. Resting on top was an open laptop and the plastic skull with a bright pink sticky note stuck to the

forehead. Otherwise, the desk was empty. There was no lesson plan, no sonnet book, nothing.

"He's gone!" moaned Lawrence.

Summer picked up the skull. "Play me," the sticky note read. It had a large black arrow in permanent marker that pointed to the laptop. Summer pressed the space key, and the screen flickered to life. A video began to play.

The students saw Mr. Finn adjusting the camera on the laptop. After focusing the lens on his face, he gave them a wave and sat back. "Hey, guys," he said. "You were right. You need a real teacher. So I'm on my way back to my old job."

The students looked at one another in dismay.

"But just so you know," continued Mr. Finn, "even though it was only a day, being your teacher was one of the greatest honors of my life." He looked down. "So I guess this is good-bye. Forever."

The students gasped. They had decided to accept Mr. Finn—only now it was too late!

But Mr. Finn had one final parting gift for them. "Oh! Check out the box," he said, pointing down with a smile.

Zack shut the laptop sadly and put it aside. The students lifted the flaps of the cardboard box and peered inside. They couldn't believe what they saw. There was a flying disc, a water gun, a poster, juggling balls, and tons more.

"Whoa!" Zack reached in and pulled out a plastic green slingshot.

Lawrence gasped and picked up a metal robot.

"Mr. Finn got all of our stuff back from the Confiscation Closet!" Summer exclaimed.

"My dodgeball!" Tomika hugged the red bouncy ball as hard as she could.

"Why'd that get taken away?" asked Freddy.

Tomika threw the dodgeball at Freddy and

hit him square in the head. She grinned. Her aim was still perfect.

Freddy rubbed his nose. "Now I get it."

Zack clenched his hand around his sling-shot. "Mr. Finn left because of us," he said. "We have to get him back if we want to be in a band."

"Absolutely," chimed in the other students.

"We'd better move fast," cautioned Tomika. "If Principal Mullins sees that he's gone, he's gonna be fired."

"Then let's get to that yogurt stand!" Summer declared.

The other students nodded in agreement.

"But how?" asked Freddy. He knew that there was at least one major threat that would prevent them from leaving the school—other than Principal Mullins. "We have to get past the hall monitor, and that kid is ruthless!"

Lawrence smiled smugly. "Don't worry, guys." He held up his rocket. "I got this."

CHAPTER 11

HANDS ON HIPS, HIS FACE FIXED IN A

permanent scowl, Clark stood before the entrance of William Travis Prep, patrolling the terrain with two suspicious eyes. His bright yellow vest gleamed with authority. Nothing escaped his watchful glare. As hall monitor, he had put more kids in detention than all of the teachers at William Travis Prep combined.

"Hall pass!" he barked as girl in a plaid dress with bright blue stockings walked down the hallway. She whirled as if she had been

stung. Trembling, she held up a large lami-
nated badge bearing the school's emblem.

Clark scrutinized the pass, looking for signs
of fraud. Finally he gave a curt nod. "You got
lucky . . . this time," he growled. "Move along."

The girl fled down the hallway.

A video camera with a rocket attached to
it came rolling down the hallway on a skateboard. Clark glanced down at it, knowing that
something was off.

Back in the classroom, the students were gathered around Lawrence's computer. Lawrence
had synced the video camera's lens with the
computer so that they could see everything
going on in the hallway. He had also hooked
the computer up to a joystick, and was con-
trolling the skateboard's every move from the
comfort of his desk.

"That's amazing, Lawrence!" said Freddy.

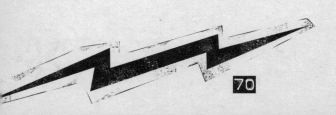

Lawrence's tech skills were finally coming in handy!

The skateboard rammed into Clark's leg. "Ow!" he yelped. He looked down and frowned. "No skateboards allowed!" he shouted. He looked around, hunting for the culprit. "Whose is this?" he demanded.

When no one responded, Clark gave an exasperated sigh and bent down to confiscate the camera rocket skateboard. As he reached for it, the skateboard jerked back. Puzzled, Clark took a step forward and reached for it again.

"Hey, Clark! Can't catch me!" chortled Lawrence back in the classroom. He loved it when his gadgets worked! He wrenched back on the joystick.

The camera backed out of Clark's range and zoomed down the hallway. It made a sharp turn, racing past yellow and blue lockers, with Clark hot on its wheels. Clark snarled as he swiped at the skateboard, missing by a few inches. He swiped again, coming even closer.

"He's gaining on you!" yelled Zack.

It was time for Lawrence to pull out his ace card. "Time to launch the rocket!" he announced. He typed quickly on the computer, setting up a few key commands.

Freddy leaned forward, squinting at the screen. He suddenly felt like maybe donating his board hadn't been the best idea. "Wait. Is my skateboard going to be okay?"

"Did I mention that there's a *rocket* strapped to it?" Lawrence rolled his eyes. "So . . . no."

As much as he loved his skateboard, Freddy knew that this was more important. "It's for Mr. Finn." He took a deep breath. "Do it."

Lawrence planted his thumb on the red button of the joystick and pressed. The students watched as the rocket exploded into action, pushing the skateboard into ultra-speed mode. Clark doubled his pace, but it still wasn't fast enough to catch Lawrence's smoking Confiscation Closet invention.

Lawrence adjusted the controls so the skateboard would keep zipping through the hallways. "That'll keep him busy." He jabbed down on the joystick one last time. "Let's go."

The students rushed out of the classroom and through the double door exit. They found their bike helmets and strapped them on as they ran down the school steps.

Next to the stairs was the bike stand where all of their bikes were parked. But when they tried to grab their bikes, none of the students could pull them free.

Freddy noticed a huge metal chain. It looped through all of the bike frames and onto the bike stand. "Someone chained our bikes together!"

"I did," said Lawrence. "It's a titanium chain with a combination code that's virtually impossible to crack." He smiled proudly, sure that his friends would thank him for keeping their bikes so safe. "You're welcome!"

"Great! What's the combination?" Zack yanked on his bike. "We're kind of in a hurry."

Lawrence opened his mouth. Then he shut it. Then he opened it again. Then he shut it again. "Um, funny thing," he said, chuckling nervously. "I . . . forgot."

"What?" cried the others. Now how were they going to get to Mr. Finn and back in time?

CHAPTER 12

"SEE? I TOLD YOU GUYS IT WOULD ALL work out," Freddy puffed.

The gang had been able to get on their bikes and leave, but not in the way they had expected. They were lined up in a row, gasping for air as they pedaled together, dragging the heavy bike stand behind them.

"Ugh," groaned Zack. He looked back to see sparks flying behind them. The bike stand was scraping against the road, creating mini fireworks as the students heaved their way forward. Zack shook his head. At least they were moving. He gritted his teeth and pedaled harder.

The students kept lumbering through the streets. Luckily none of the cars seemed to mind driving around a line of five bikes. Finally, they turned a corner and pulled up to Sixth Street. They could see the yogurt stand ahead of them, a sad white metal freezer with a blue and white umbrella hanging above it.

"Here we are!" Freddy hopped off his bike.

Lawrence snapped his fingers. "I just remembered the combination!" he said triumphantly.

Summer gave him an exasperated look.

"Well, no harm done," said Lawrence cheerfully.

The gang dismounted and took off their helmets. None of them turned to see what the bike stand had snagged along the way— overturned garbage cans, bouquets of flowers, and traffic cones were piled in a heap on top

of the stand. A red inflatable waving air man bobbed up and down over the gigantic mess.

More than one onlooker stopped to take in the sight of five middle schoolers who had dragged a bike stand across town. But the students didn't even notice. They had more important things on their minds.

"There's Mr. Finn!" cried Tomika. She barely recognized him. He was dressed in brown tights and white sneakers, wearing a vanilla yogurt costume. The brown ribbed cloth of the cone hung over his lower half, while white swirls of vanilla dotted with red, yellow, and blue sprinkles covered his upper half. He wore a pointy hat covered in more sprinkles, and was holding two cones dripping with frozen vanilla yogurt. He did not look happy.

The gang dropped their bikes with a clatter and rushed to their teacher.

"Two sugar cones," Mr. Finn intoned to a bored-looking woman and a guy with huge hair. "Yo, yo, yo. My name is Yogurt Boy," he sang, waving the cones listlessly from side to side. "Dishing out the yizzle, for you to enjoy." He tried to do some dancing jumping jacks, but then just gave up and handed the customers their cones.

After collecting his money, Mr. Finn turned to see Freddy, Tomika, Summer, Zack, and Lawrence staring at him. Their mouths were open.

"Hey guys." Mr. Finn was about to ask the students what was going on and if they wanted some yogurt, when he stopped. "Wait." He put his hands on his hips and looked at them as sternly as he could. "Why aren't you in school?"

Tomika sheepishly ran her hand through her hair. She wanted Mr. Finn to go back to being their teacher, but now that it was time

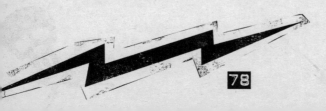

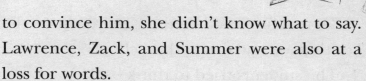

to convince him, she didn't know what to say. Lawrence, Zack, and Summer were also at a loss for words.

Freddy spoke for the group. "We want you to come back, Mr. Finn."

"Yeah," the other students cheered. They waited for what seemed like eons for Mr. Finn to reply.

Mr. Finn shook his head. "I can't go back. I have my dignity." He looked down at his frozen yogurt suit and sighed. "Besides, you guys are right. You need a real teacher."

Summer went over and put a hand on Mr. Finn's yogurty arm. "You *are* a real teacher, Mr. Finn!"

"Yeah!" the others agreed.

"I mean, you taught us the meaning of Shakespeare!" Summer continued. "You inspired us to rock out in the quad, and you made learning fun."

"Actual fun!" said Freddy. "Do you know the last time we had fun at that school?"

The students tried to think back.

"Kindergarten. December twelfth," Tomika said finally, a faraway look in her eyes. "Finger painting." She noticed the others were looking at her. "It really doesn't happen much," she said with a shrug.

"Yeah," Zack sighed wistfully.

"C'mon, Mr. Finn," said Freddy. "We want to win Battle of the Bands."

The other students nodded.

"And we can't do it without you," said Freddy.

"Pleeeeeaaaassseee?" pleaded Lawrence.

Summer could see that Mr. Finn was beginning to waver. She had an idea. Maybe bargaining with Mr. Finn would work. "You want to be a teacher, and we want to be a rock band," she said.

Mr. Finn nodded. "Yeah."

"We'll make you a deal," Summer proposed. "We'll keep your secret, if you keep ours."

"C'mon, Mr. Finn," said Freddy.

"Come back with us!" begged Tomika.

"Pleeeeeaaaassseee?" repeated Lawrence. This time, Zack joined in, too.

Mr. Finn looked uncertain. There was a long silence. The kids held their breath and crossed their fingers. They had no clue what Mr. Finn was going to say.

Then, a huge smile broke out over Mr. Finn's face. "You got yourselves a deal!" he shouted.

"Yes!" cheered the gang.

CHAPTER 13

"C'MON, PEDAL HARDER!" MR. FINN

cried as the students biked back to the school. After agreeing to come back with them, he had ditched his yogurt costume and put his teacher's blazer back on. But before leaving his uncle's frozen yogurt stand, he had given everyone a large cone with extra sprinkles.

The yogurt was delicious, but it was very hard for the students to eat it while staying upright on their bikes. It didn't help that their bikes were still chained to the bike stand, which was collecting even more street debris. In classic fashion, Lawrence had forgotten the combination to his titanium chain lock—again.

"We've got to get back to school before we get caught!" Mr. Finn grinned and took a bite out of his yogurt.

"Ugh," Tomika groaned. She was huffing and puffing and pedaling with all her might. It wasn't just the weight of the bike stand that was making this ride back to school tough. Since Mr. Finn didn't have a bike, he now sat comfortably on her handlebars, nibbling on his cone while she pedaled furiously. "Shouldn't this be the other way around?" she asked her teacher.

"Nah." Mr. Finn crossed his legs happily and took another bite off the top of his yogurt scoop. "This feels right."

After what seemed like ages, the gang finally made it back to school. They leapt off their bikes, licked the last smudges of yogurt from their faces, and hurtled down the hallway, with Mr. Finn in the lead. They froze, though, when they saw a familiar dreaded shape blocking their way.

Principal Mullins stood with her back toward them. She had one pink earbud plugged into her ear and was bopping her head to the music. Then Principal Mullins must have heard a suspicious noise over the song. She started to turn her head. If she turned it any farther, she would have caught the entire class outside of the classroom.

Mr. Finn silently motioned for the students to shuffle right, out of view from the principal's stern eyes.

Principal Mullins turned her head the other way. The students jerked to a stop and shuffled left.

Principal Mullins shrugged. She popped the remaining earbud into her other ear and went back listening to her music. As the chorus swelled, she started to swing her hips.

Lawrence's cheeks puffed out. Watching their strict principal getting her groove on was more than he could handle. But before he could laugh, Freddy wrapped his hand around Lawrence's mouth. Summer looked on, terrified that Lawrence would give them away.

But Freddy had caught the laugh in time.

Strutting like a model on an imaginary runway, Principal Mullins shoved open the double doors leading to the classrooms. Shaking her booty and waving her hand like a cowgirl lassoing a bull, she disappeared out of sight.

There was an uncomfortable silence.

"You can't unsee that," moaned Tomika.

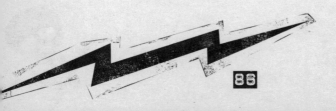

Knowing they had just a few seconds before they would be caught, Mr. Finn motioned for the students to follow him. They raced down the hallway, took a hard left, and burst through their classroom door. Mr. Finn hastily grabbed a science textbook from the teacher's desk and yanked it open as the students piled into their seats, just seconds before Principal Mullins entered the classroom.

"And that explains space. And time," Mr. Finn told the class, pretending that he had just finished up with their lesson. He snapped the textbook closed, stealthily double-checking to make sure that the textbook was facing right side up. He gave a tiny sigh of relief when he saw that it was.

"I just dropped by to see how things were going," said Principal Mullins.

Summer raised her hand. "I think I can

speak for all of us when I say that learning from Mr. Finn has been quite an adventure."

"Well." Principal Mullins tapped her notebook. "I see you have things under control."

Mr. Finn gave her a thumbs-up.

"Keep up the good work," Principal Mullins told him, and shut the classroom door.

Everyone breathed a sigh of relief. Lawrence ran over to the door and lifted up one of the maroon blinds covering the glass window. "She's gone!"

"All right, then." Mr. Finn clapped his hands together. "Battle of the Bands is coming up, and we got a lot of work to do." He tossed his head back, and his hair went flying. "Let's rock!"

It didn't take long before the students had transformed their classroom back into a rock concert stage. Summer grabbed the tambourine while Lawrence scrambled to the keyboard. Tomika, Zack, and Mr. Finn slung on guitars. Freddy eagerly took his place behind the drum set. With amps on, guitars plugged in, tambourine poised, and drumsticks at the ready, the gang got ready to rock and roll.

Mr. Finn switched on his guitar and nodded to Freddy. Freddy hit his drumsticks together. He knew exactly what to play. "One, two, three, four!"

The Romantics song "What I Like About You" pounded through the air as Freddy, Tomika, Summer, Zack, Lawrence, and Mr. Finn rocked on. They powered through the song with even more energy than they had at the recital. The electricity pulsed through the room as the kids and Mr. Finn all had the time of their lives.

As the song came to an end, stage fireworks lit up the room. Mr. Finn jumped and threw his hands in the air, rocker style. The gang cheered and high fived. They couldn't wait to learn how to rock with Mr. Finn. And when it came time for the Battle of the Bands, they knew they would be ready.